MR. NOBODY

by Roger Hargreaves

Original story by
Roger Hargreaves

Illustrated by **Roger Hargreaves**
and **Adam Hargreaves**

EGMONT

Hello!

Meet Mr Happy.

Happy by name, and happy by nature.

And now, I'm going to tell you a story.

Actually, this isn't a story about Mr Happy.

Well, not really.

It's about somebody he met, not very long ago.

Last month, in fact.

Mr Happy had been to tea with Little Miss Sunshine.

He thought about catching a bus to take him home. But, as it was such a nice day, he thought again, and decided to walk.

And he was glad he did!

Would you like to know why?

I shan't tell you!

Not yet, anyway.

Mr Happy was whistling to himself as he walked along, when he heard a noise.

He stopped.

There it was again!

A sort of sniffing noise.

SNIFF! SNIFF! SNIFF!

Suddenly, a drop of rain splashed on top of his head.

"That's odd," he thought to himself, looking up. "There isn't a cloud in the sky!"

And then – he couldn't believe his eyes.

You'll never guess what Mr Happy saw.

There, sitting on the branch of a tree, was somebody who sort of was, but wasn't!

I know it sounds ridiculous, but it's true.

You could see through him!

And he was crying real big fat wet tears.

Which, of course, were what had splashed on top of Mr Happy's head.

"Who," Mr Happy managed to splutter, "are you?"

The person who sort of was, but wasn't, looked mournfully down at him, and, in a mournful, melancholy voice, replied, "Nobody."

"Nobody?" gasped Mr Happy. "But everybody's somebody!"

The person who sort of was, but wasn't, sighed deeply.

"Except me," he said. And he started to cry more real big fat wet tears.

Mr Happy scratched his head, which was getting quite wet by this time.

"Can you get down?" he wondered.

"Possibly," replied Mr Nobody. And he climbed down out of the tree.

"Where have you come from?" asked Mr Happy.

"Nowhere." Mr Nobody sighed the sort of sigh that breaks your heart.

"I know I used to be somebody. But I can't remember who!" He sniffed. "Or what!" He sniffed. "Or where!" He sniffed. "Or when!" He sobbed.

Mr Happy couldn't help but stare. It isn't often you meet somebody you can see right through!

"I think," said Mr Happy, "that you had better come home with me."

"Why?" sobbed Mr Nobody.

"Because," said Mr Happy, "we must do something about you."

"There's nothing you can do about a nobody," wept the person who sort of was, but wasn't.

"Of course there is," said Mr Happy. "Follow me!"

Eventually, they reached Mr Happy's house, and went into his living room.

Mr Happy pointed to a chair.

"Sit yourself down," he said.

It was really quite extraordinarily extraordinary seeing somebody who was nobody sitting in a chair.

Mr Happy sat down too.

And thought. Hard!

"The wizard!" cried Mr Happy. "Of course!"

So, the following morning, after no breakfast, Mr Happy took Mr Nobody to see the wizard.

"Ah!" remarked the wizard, after Mr Happy had tried to explain.

"Ah!" he said again, eyeing Mr Nobody.

Mr Nobody just stood there, looking as glum as anyone can look.

Just try turning the corners of your mouth down as far as they will go. Go on!

Well, that's about half as glum as Mr Nobody looked.

The wizard thought and thought.

And thought some more.

"Care for a cup of tea?" he enquired.

"Nobodys don't drink nothing," replied Mr Nobody.

"Nobodys don't drink ANYthing," said the wizard, correcting him.

"That's right," agreed Mr Nobody.

"Aha!" cried the wizard. "That's it!"

The wizard rushed over to his workbench, and started to mix up lots of different coloured liquids in a huge bottle.

They bubbled and gurgled together, and let off little puffs of white smoke.

BUBBLE! BUBBLE! GURGLE! PUFF!

BUBBLE! BUBBLE! GURGLE! PUFF!

"What colour would you like to be?" the wizard asked Mr Nobody.

"Nobodys aren't coloured," came the sad reply.

"You choose!" said the wizard, pointing at Mr Happy.

Mr Happy thought.

"Well," he said, "I've always really rather quite enjoyed being yellow."

"YELLOW IT SHALL BE!" shouted the wizard, as he poured more liquid into the bottle.

Suddenly, with one huge PUFF! of white smoke,
the liquid turned bright yellow!

"Right!" cried the wizard. "Drink that!"

"Nobodys don't drink nothing," said Mr Nobody.

"EXACTLY," shouted the wizard, at the top of his voice.
"NOBODYS DON'T DRINK NOTHING! THEREFORE,
NOBODYS MUST DRINK SOMETHING!"

Mr Nobody took hold of the bottle, and took
a small sip.

"MORE!" cried the wizard. "Much MORE!"

Mr Nobody shut his eyes.

And took a deep breath.

And, swallowed all of the liquid!

Mr Happy and the wizard watched and waited,
and waited and watched.

Nothing happened!

"Told you so," said Mr Nobody.

And he sighed, another one of those sighs that break
your heart.

But – wait a minute!

Did their eyes deceive them, or –

They looked at Mr Nobody's feet.

They were turning sort of, yes, yellow!

Yes! Decidedly yellow!

Definitely yellow!

Then Mr Nobody's legs turned yellow!

And then his body!

And then his arms!

"His nose!" Mr Happy shouted. "What about his nose?"

They watched and they waited. And they waited and they watched.

Nothing happened!

Suddenly, Mr Nobody sneezed!

And, immediately after he sneezed, with an enormous

POP! AtishooPOP!

his nose turned yellow as well!

Oh, I wish you'd been there to see Mr Nobody's face.

His mouth stopped turning down, and started turning up.

And up, and up, and up again!

"Well," chuckled Mr Happy, "I told you so –

– everybody's a SOMEBODY!"

Fantastic offers for Mr. Men fans!

Collect all your
Mr. Men or Little Miss books in these superb durable collector's cases!

Only £5.99 inc. postage and packaging, these wipe clean, hard wearing cases will give all your Mr. Men and Little Miss books a beautiful new home!

STICK £1
COIN HERE
(For poster only)

Keep track of your favourite
Mr. Men and Little Miss characters with this brilliant collector's poster, now featuring Mr. Nobody!

Collect 6 tokens and we will send you a giant-sized double-sided poster! Simply tape a £1 coin in the space provided and fill out the form overleaf.

Only need a few Mr. Men or Little Miss to complete your set? You can order any of the titles on the back of the books from our Mr. Men order line on 0870 787 1724. The majority of orders are delivered in 5 to 7 working days.

--- **TO BE COMPLETED BY AN ADULT** ---

To apply for any of these great offers, ask an adult to complete the details below and send this whole page with the appropriate payment and tokens, to: MR. MEN CLASSIC OFFER PO BOX 715, HORSHAM RH12 5WG

[ ] Please send me a giant-sized double-sided collector's poster.

AND [ ] I enclose 6 tokens and have taped a £1 coin to the other side of this page

[ ] Please send me [ ] Mr. Men Library case(s) and/or [ ] Little Miss Library case(s) at £5.99 each inc P&P

[ ] I enclose a cheque/postal order payable to Egmont UK Limited for £............

OR [ ] Please debit my MasterCard / Visa / Maestro / Delta account (delete as appropriate) for £............

Card no. [ ][ ][ ][ ][ ][ ][ ][ ][ ][ ][ ][ ][ ][ ][ ][ ][ ][ ] Security code [ ][ ][ ]

Issue no. (if available) [ ] Start Date [ ][ ] / [ ][ ] / [ ][ ] Expiry Date [ ][ ] / [ ][ ] / [ ][ ]

Fan's name: .... Date of birth: ....

Address: ....

....

Postcode: ....

Name of parent / guardian: ....

Email of parent / guardian: ....

Signature of parent / guardian